James the Vine Puller

A Brazilian folktale retold by Martha Bennett Stiles

Illustrations by Larry Thomas

Carolrhoda Books, Inc./Minneapolis

To my nice niece and good goddaughter,
Christina Jeanne Wells

This edition first published 1992 by Carolrhoda Books, Inc.

Library of Congress Cataloging-in-Publication Data

Stiles, Martha Bennett.
  James the vine puller : a Brazilian folktale / retold by Martha
Bennett Stiles ; illustrations by Larry Thomas.
       p.   cm.
  Summary: A retelling of the Brazilian version of an African folk-
tale in which a turtle outsmarts both an elephant and a whale.
  ISBN 0-897614-775-9
  [1. Folklore—Brazil. 2. Animals—Folklore.] I. Thomas, Larry. ill.
II. Title.
PZ8.1.S8575Jam 1992
398.24'52'0981—dc20
[E]   92-2790
                                                            CIP
                                                            AC

Manufactured in the United States of America

1 2 3 4 5 6 97 96 95 94 93 92

Introduction

Folktales are stories that families and friends tell over and over again. When people travel to different countries, they bring their favorite stories along. Soon people in the new country are telling these stories, too. This is how *James the Vine Puller* became a Brazilian folktale.

In the 1500s, people from Portugal came to the land now known as Brazil. They found that it was a good place to grow sugar, and they forced the Arawak people and others who lived there to work as slaves on their sugar plantations. Many of these native people died from diseases and hard work. So the Portuguese brought people from Africa to be slaves. Life was very hard for these slaves, but one way to make the time pass and to remember their own country was to tell stories. Africans brought the story of James the Vine Puller to Brazil.

Now this story is told by Brazilians, too. But you can still see the African parts of the story. There are no wild elephants in Brazil, so the elephant in this story is African. And James, the turtle, plays tricks on other animals just like the tricky tortoise in many African folktales.

For the Arawak people of Brazil, this folktale became a way to explain high and low tides on an ocean—why sometimes the water of the ocean comes up high on the shore and sometimes it stays low. But no matter what country you're from, you'll love this story about James and his vine-pulling adventure....

Once, in the jungles of Brazil, there lived a turtle
named James. He lived under the palm trees, with
orchids blooming all around him. His favorite foods
were coconuts and seaweed. Mornings, he played on
the beach and went swimming. Evenings, he watched
the beautiful sunsets over the ocean. Life was good.

One evening while James was eating a coconut for supper, the earth rumbled under him, the leaves of the jungle bushes parted, and there stood…a mighty elephant!

"What are you doing, eating coconuts from *my* tree?" the elephant roared. "I am the king of the jungle, and everything in the jungle is *mine.*" The elephant wrapped his trunk around the tree and shook it furiously. Coconuts fell so fast James had to scurry for his life.

James decided to find his supper in the ocean instead. He swam out to some floating seaweed. It was very tasty, and James began to feel more cheerful.

Suddenly the waves became so large that they washed him right up on the shore. Then out of the ocean rose a huge black shape. It was a whale!

"What is this?" the whale said softly. "Were you *really* stealing from my ocean garden?" The great whale sighed. "I would like you to have all the seaweed you want. It is too bad there is not enough to go around. But what is the use of being king of the ocean if *I* do

not have all that *I* want?" He looked at James with his
little eyes and said, "I am sorry, but if I notice you in
my garden again, I will have to drown you."

With that, the whale waved his tail and vanished
under the water.

"Dear me," James said to himself. "There seem to be quite a few kings around here. I suppose if I could fly into the sky and eat those cotton-candy clouds, some king would swoop down and offer to peck my eyes out!"

James went to bed hungry that night—but the next morning he had a plan.

First he found the elephant. "You are a very selfish
king," James said bravely. "What if I took your crown
away from you?"

The elephant snorted. "A little thing like you?" He
rippled his muscles and stamped his great feet on the
ground.

"I may be little," said James, "but I'm not afraid to challenge you to a vine-pulling contest. If I win, you must leave the jungle. If you win, I will go away."

The elephant thought what fun it would be to pull this little turtle around by a vine. He agreed to join in the contest that very afternoon.

Then James sent a crab into the ocean to find the whale.

After a while the big hump of the whale rose slowly above the water. He looked down at the little turtle sitting on the sand and said, "So it was you who sent for me. *Please*, how can I serve you?"

"I would like to be king of the ocean for a while," James replied. "I challenge you to a vine-pulling contest. If I win, you must find another ocean to rule. If I lose, I will never come into your water again."

The whale had been awakened from his morning nap. "My friend," he replied, "I would like nothing better." He was thinking about how he would pull that little turtle halfway around the world.

"Then give me your tail," said James. "I will tie one end of the vine to your tail and the other end to my leg. When I have walked until the vine is pulled tight, I will tug on the vine. That will be the signal for the contest to begin. We will see who can pull harder and be king of this ocean!"

James began walking, but when he was behind the trees he took the vine off his leg. He carried the vine to the elephant, who was waiting for him.

"It's time for our contest," he said to the elephant. "I will tie this vine to your trunk. Then I will go to the other end of the vine and tie it to my leg. When I give the vine a jerk, that will be the signal for you to start pulling."

The elephant smiled broadly and waited while James walked back toward the ocean. As soon as the elephant couldn't see him anymore, James gave the vine a jerk and hid behind a palm tree.

The whale pulled on one end of the vine and the elephant pulled on the other end.

When the whale pulled, he almost dragged the elephant into the water. But since the whale was under the water, the elephant thought it was the turtle on the other end of the vine.

Then the elephant used all his strength and almost drew the whale up on the shore. But since the elephant was behind the trees, the whale *also* thought the turtle was on the other end of the vine.

The two kings struggled back and forth all afternoon.

At last when they were both too tired to move, James came out of hiding. He said to the elephant, "I see that neither of us can win this contest. So let us each agree to live—and eat—in the jungle as before."

The elephant, panting for breath and hanging his head in shame, agreed to make peace.

Then James went to the whale. "You see that you are no stronger than I," said James. "Perhaps we should agree to leave each other alone."

"Perhaps we should," whispered the tired whale, and he never bothered James again.

James went back to eating coconuts and seaweed, and taking morning swims. There was peace in the jungle, and the orchids and sunsets had never been so beautiful as they were that season.